Present for Peace

Experience the Gift of Peace Being Present

A free parent / teacher guide for this book
can be downloaded at Present for Peace

www.presentforpeace.com

Published by Present for Peace
© 2023 by Cindy Olejar

To contact the author you may email Cindy Olejar at presentforpeace@gmail.com.

ISBN (hardback): 979-8-9878432-0-8
ISBN (paperback): 979-8-9878432-1-5
ISBN (ebook): 979-8-9878432-2-2

Illustrations by Jess Bircham

Book Design by Arlene Soto, Intricate Designs

Being present with uncomfortable feelings

Beach Day Blues for Wally

Written by Cindy Olejar

Illustrated by Jess Bircham

Wally eagerly watched the sun going down.

He was so excited because tomorrow was the first time this summer his family could take a trip to the beach.

When nighttime finally came, Wally lay in bed but was having a hard time falling asleep thinking about the beach. He couldn't wait to swim, picnic and play in the sand.

Exhausted from the anticipation of the beach day,
Wally finally fell asleep.

But when he woke up the next morning, Wally heard a gentle tapping sound of rain and saw water streaming down his window.

Wally's heart sank. "This is not fair!
I want to be at the beach today."

Wally dragged himself out of bed and went to the living room where he found his brother Donny reading comic books.

He wished he was reading under a cool towel fort he made at the beach.

He saw his sister Amy playing with sand art.

He wished he was playing in the real sand at the beach.

"Good morning, Wally. I'm sorry the rain canceled our beach day. Would you like to help make breakfast for everyone?" Dad asked.
"No, thank you."

He'd rather be at the beach having a picnic.

"I want the sun to come out. Rainy days are boring."

Feeling tired and defeated, even though he had not been physically active, Wally threw himself onto his bed careful not to disturb Murphy, the family cat. "This whole day is ruined, Murphy!"

Wally noticed how peaceful Murphy looked.
He could feel Murphy's soft and slow breath on
the back of his hand.

He could also sense how relaxed Murphy's body felt when petting him.

Wally then closed his eyes and paid attention to his own breath. Wally's breathing began to slow down. His body began to relax.

The disappointment he was feeling even faded.

When Wally opened his eyes, he noticed his swimsuit hanging on a chair. Distracting thoughts came back. He was not going to the beach today.

A feeling of sadness came. His breathing quickened. His face and hands tensed.

He also felt angry that going to the
beach may not happen at all this summer!

Wally closed his eyes again and
went back to observing his breath.

Again his breathing slowed down.

His body relaxed.

And the uncomfortable feelings faded.

Feeling much more relaxed, Wally opened his eyes.
He looked around his room. This time he noticed
things he hadn't been paying attention to before.
He'd been too focused on what he couldn't have.

He saw his magic cards, books, rock collection, drum, basketball, journal and colored pencils. He saw his boots, his hat, his raincoat and his gloves.

Still aware of his breathing, when he looked out the window he didn't see the rain as something bad anymore. "Hey Mom!" Wally suddenly called out.

Mom came to Wally's bedroom door.
"What's going on?"

"If I wear my rain gear, could I ask my
friend Mason to come over to play outside?"
"Yes, that's a great idea!" replied his mom.

Wally and Mason had a great time splashing in puddles,

listening to the rain tap the leaves,

and catching raindrops in their mouths.

They even spotted an
owl in a tree!

Dad said, "Looks like you found a way to be at peace with the rainy day, Wally."

"Yeah, the rain stopped us from going to the beach today, but once I welcomed the rain I started to see what was here."

CPSIA information can be obtained
at www.ICGtesting.com
Printed in the USA
LVHW080720150523
746776LV00003B/11